IF WISHES WERE SAABS

To Vicki —
With fondest memories
of a sunny summer ...
and other sweet moments.
May all your wishes come
true. Tom Davleysh

Stefan Underhill

IF WISSHES WERE SAABS

and other nursery rhymes for modern times

Tom Darbyshire & Stefan Underhill

Illustrated by Carol M. Vidinghoff

LITTLE, BROWN AND COMPANY

BOSTON   TORONTO

LIBRARY OF CONGRESS CATALOG CARD NO. 85-81557

FIRST EDITION

*Thanks to: Mary Pat, Shawn, Dave, Shannon, Chris, Claire
Dion, our families, friends at the U and everybody who gives
up a trip to Häagen Dazs to buy this book.*

RRD

DESIGNED BY JEANNE F. ABBOUD

*Published simultaneously in Canada
by Little, Brown & Company (Canada) Limited*

PRINTED IN THE UNITED STATES OF AMERICA

To Mariah,

who was born about the same time as this book.
May her life be upwardly mobile.

If Wishes Were Saabs

If wishes were Saabs,
    All Type A's would ride.
If wishes were timeshares,
    They'd summer seaside.
If Type A's were Type B's,
    They'd wish a lot less;
And die of old age,
    Instead of from stress.

Mary Had a Little Land

Mary had a little land
   To lease for lots of dough,
But every room that Mary let
   The tenant out she'd throw.

She signed a lease with John one day,
   His job she did not know,
And when he couldn't pay the rent,
   Of course, he had to go.

She rented to some college kids
   Who came from Ohio,
But pretty soon she kicked them out—
   Them and their stereo.

The next renters seemed ideal,
   A couple, newly wed,
Until they sprang a king-size leak
   In their queen-size waterbed.

The next chap was a gentleman
   Quite cultured and urbane…
Who'd think that he'd get busted
   For dealing in cocaine?

Now Mary's sold her property
   But there's no cause to frown.
She made a killing on the deal,
   'Cause she'd read *Nothing Down*.

There Was a Young Woman

There was a young woman,
  Didn't know what to do:
She wanted to have kids
  And keep working too.
She just couldn't face
  Stepping off the fast track
So she hired a nanny,
  Took six weeks, and came back.

Little Jack Horner

Little Jack Horner
    The market did corner
With futures on the live hog crop.
    But his plan was killed
    When the contracts were filled
And they brought the hogs to his co-op.

Six million head of pork
    Were sent to New York,
To the Horner address came the swine.
    Jack's plan's up in smoke
    And now he's flat broke,
But he brings home the bacon just fine.

Simple Simon

Simple Simon spent some time on
    The science of raising a tot.
Said Simple Simon, "The task that I'm on
    Deserves my very best shot."

So Simon read with increasing dread
    Some books like Dr. Spock's.
He learned of breast-feeding,
Of rashes and breeding
    And prepared for the coming shocks.

When babe arrived, Simon dived
    To count each finger and toe
(This vital stat was a detail that
    The sonogram didn't show).

The baby's birth brought Simon mirth—
    A miracle of biology.
He would not rest till she had the best
    In kiddie-care technology.

Now Simon knew "just toys" won't do—
    "My tot needs stimulation!"
He had to find some toys "DESIGNED
    BY EXPERTS OF EDUCATION."

These high-tech toys make special noise,
    Are colored bright red and blue;
They bounce and shake,
But will not break;
    They're chewable, nontoxic, too.

For mental advancements,
Toys have enhancements
    That titillate body and soul,
While other toys try
To sync hand and eye
    Through the proper shake,
Rattle, and roll.

And Simon found to get around
    In strollers babes should ride.
So Simon went and a fortune spent
    To transport tot with pride.

With swivel wheels and locking heels
   His Aprica really moved.
Its bumper guard of rubber hard
   Is EPA Approved.

Next a nursery set and bassinet
   With lots of lacy frills;
Then to work he beat a quick retreat
   So he could pay the bills.

But he felt bereft if he merely left
   Babe under a mobile with chimes,
So with her he'd play
For an hour each day—
   And call it "quality time."

Früsen Gladje

(To the tune of "Frère Jacques")

Früsen Gladje, Früsen Gladje,
Häagen Dazs, Häagen Dazs,
Sorbet and Tofutti,
Name them to sound snooty,
They'll sell well,
They'll sell well.

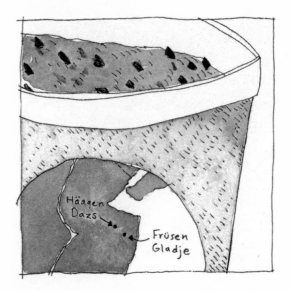

Young Mother Hubbard

Young Mother Hubbard
Went to the cupboard
   To get her new baby a meal.
But when she got there,
She found choosing the fare
   To be a task *très difficile.*

In Hubbard's cupboard, no signs
Of Gerber or Heinz,
   And Beech-Nut? Oh no, too *passé.*
Instead there were jars
Of cuisine fit for czars—
   Hubbard Junior ate strictly gourmet.

On the first shelf there were
Strained Scampi *à beurre*.
   Looking upward the second was filled
With jars stacked so neat
Of Minced Mignon Mesquite
   And Salmon Mini-Mousse, lightly dilled.

In the very top jars?
Kiddy Caviars…
   Strained Sushi…Coquettes au Vin…
Kinder Kiwi Puree…
Tins of Petite Pâté…
   And portions of Goo Goo Gai Pan.

Thus Junior was raised
And spent his young days
   A-nibbling on life's little plums.
For life is a feast—
It is, at least,
   When you're born silver spoon
'Twixt your gums.

Hush, Little Baby

Hush, little baby,
Don't say a thing,
Daddy's gonna buy you
A Tiffany teething ring.
If that teething ring
Makes you bored,
How 'bout a baby bottle
From Waterford?
If that crystal bottle
Leaves you blank,
Perhaps a sterling silver
Neiman-Marcus piggy bank?
If that piggy bank
Doesn't suit your whim,
Daddy will buy you
Some shares of IBM.
If those stock shares
Don't drive you wild,
Daddy will wonder
If you're really his child.

Solomon Grundy

Solomon Grundy
Went to Yale on Monday,
Law degree on Tuesday,
Took the bar on Wednesday,
Joined the firm on Thursday,
Partner on Friday,
Heart attack on Saturday,
Buried on Sunday.
That was the end
Of Solomon Grundy.

Little Bo-Peep

Little Bo-Peep divorced that creep—
　　She thought that she would get her
Another spouse, less of a louse,
　　Whose cash was flowing better.

She called around, but Bo-Peep found
　　Commitment made men wary.
And those not gay were content to play—
　　They simply would not marry.

She reached down deep, did little Bo-Peep,
　　And told herself emphatically:
"Devise a plan to catch a man
　　And follow it systematically."

Now, just like you young Bo-Peep knew
　　She didn't need a book
To understand the task at hand—
　　You must know where to look.

Modern-day stars don't frequent bars,
     At discos won't be spied.
The one sure way to find love today
     Is through a classified.

She bought some space, an ad to place
     Within the *Village Voice.*
She chose her words to discourage nerds;
     The man she sought was choice.

"DWF, 38, seeks caring sensitive mate.
     If you're tired of frequenting dives,
Try my rowing machine and nouvelle cuisine;
     We'll share Mozart and maybe our lives."

And here, my friends, the story ends:
     She'll search for love no more,
For Little Bo-Peep hooked a corporate veep
     Making one mill' four.

Jack Sprat

Jack Sprat would eat no fat,
    His wife would eat no salt,
And any food with additives
    Was instantly at fault.

The merest hint of chemicals
    Would send them into panic
(Jacks works at Union Carbide,
    But their life-style is organic).

In their pantry? Nothing processed.
    In their cupboard? Nothing canned.
Their espresso? Never instant.
    And their pasta? Made by hand.

They'd no sooner dress their kids up
    In clothes of polyester,
Than put them in the hands
    Of a day-care child molester.

And each day they sip Perrier
    Then step out to embark
On a healthy little jog
    Through smoggy Central Park.

The Bod That Jack Built

This is the bod that Jack built.

This is the book
That extols the bod that Jack built.

This is the special low-fat grub
Explained in the book
That extols the bod that Jack built.

This is the trendy downtown club
That promotes the special low-fat grub
Explained in the book
That extols the bod that Jack built.

This is the shiny Nautilus
That sits in the trendy downtown club
That promotes the special low-fat grub
Explained in the book
That extols the bod that Jack built.

This is the corporate uppercrust
That meets by the shiny Nautilus
That sits in the trendy downtown club
That promotes the special low-fat grub
Explained in the book
That extols the bod that Jack built.

These are the new designer sweats
Worn by the corporate uppercrust
That meets by the shiny Nautilus
That sits in the trendy downtown club
That promotes the special low-fat grub
Explained in the book
That extols the bod that Jack built.

These are the nearly bouncing checks
That paid for the new designer sweats
Worn by the corporate uppercrust
That meets by the shiny Nautilus
That sits in the trendy downtown club
That promotes the special low-fat grub
Explained in the book
That extols the bod that Jack built.

Hush-a-bye-MBA

Hush-a-bye MBA, at the decision tree top,
When the wind blows, the market will drop.
When the market drops, your profits will fall,
Down will come MBA, diploma, and all.

Starlight, Starbright

Starlight, starbright
   Haven't seen a star all night.
I guess I must—perhaps I might
   Come back to Spago another night.

London's Pound
Is Falling Down

London's pound is falling down,
    Falling down, falling down;
Deals abroad do so abound—
    My, what bargains!

Off to Harrods we must fly,
    We must fly, we must fly;
There some English goods to buy—
    My, what bargains!

Look out for those VATs,
   VATs, VATs,
When in the trenches at Burberrys—
   My, what bargains!

Next to Sweden we will go,
   We will go, we will go,
To bring home a new Volvo—
   My, what bargains!

Let's forget our trip to Maine,
   Trip to Maine, trip to Maine;
Why not go instead to Spain?
   My, what bargains!

Swiss and French francs, watch them fall,
   Watch them fall, watch them fall;
Watch the dollar crush them all—
   My, what bargains!

Jane, Jane, Go Away

Jane, Jane, go away,
Let's have sex another day—
I'm too tired from work to play.

Jane, Jane, I'm too weak,
Tomorrow I must be at my peak—
Besides, we did it just last week.

Hickory-Dickory-Dock

Hickory-dickory-dock,
The biological clock:
It comes alive at thirty-five,
Hickory-dickory-dock.

Hickory-dickory-dee,
Let's have a family
And live in the land of the mini-van,
Hickory-dickory-dee.

Hickory-dickory-dum,
Full circle we'll have come,
From "Me" to "We" to "Baby-Makes-Three,"
Hickory-dickory-dum.

Hickory-dickory-dup,
We'll soon be getting up
For fairy-tale readings and midnight feedings,
Hickory-dickory-dup.

Hickory-dickory-dash,
We'll soon be spending cash
For disposable diapers and Wet-Ones wipers,
Hickory-dickory-dash.

Hickory-dickory-doe,
It's time now, don't you know,
To invest our bucks in Tonka trucks,
Hickory-dickory-doe.

Hickory-dickory-di,
Who can tell me why
Tiny shoes and such can cost so much?
Hickory-dickory-di.

Hickory-dickory-dock,
The biological clock:
It gives women cravings and blows your savings,
Hickory-dickory-dock.

She Sells Shares Short

She sells shares short
Down by the seashore,
   Stock shares she
   Sells short by the sea.
Selling stock shares short
Down by the seashore
   Outshines selling shares at Shearson,
   Don't you agree?

Tom, Tom, the Banker's Son

Tom, Tom, the banker's son
Never found time to get wash done.
But now his life is hassle-free
He found a Chinese laundry.

One, Two, Gucci Shoe

One, two,
   Gucci shoe.
Three, four,
   Christian Dior.
Five, six, seven, eight,
   Nipon's nifty, Gloria's great.
Nine then ten,
   Ralph Lauren.
Twelve, of course, comes after eleven,
   Picone, of course, comes after Evan.
Thirteen, fourteen, and fifteen,
   Something chic from Geoffrey Beene.
Fifteen, sixteen, seventeen, or so,
   Haute couture from Giorgio.
Eighteen, nineteen, now comes twenty,
Let's go home now—we've spent plenty!

Peter, Peter, Corporate Leader

Peter, Peter, corporate leader,
   Had a wife who loved the theater.
He had his corp support the arts
   So she could lunch with artsy farts.

I Know a Young Lady

I know a young lady
Who bought new shoes;
To cure her blues,
She bought new shoes.
Her charge she used.

I know a young lady
Who bought new hose
That prettied and pampered her
Down to her toes.
She bought the hose
To go with the shoes;
To cure her blues,
She bought new shoes.
Her charge she used.

I know a young lady
Who bought a new skirt—
The cost of it hurt,
But she bought a new skirt.
She bought the skirt
To go with the hose

That prettied and pampered her
Down to her toes.
She bought the hose
To go with the shoes;
To cure her blues,
She bought new shoes.
Her charge she used.

I know a young lady
Who bought a new blouse—
You could buy a small house
For the cost of that blouse.
She bought the blouse
To accent the skirt;
She bought the skirt
To go with the hose
That prettied and pampered her
Down to her toes.
She bought the hose
To go with the shoes;
To cure her blues,
She bought new shoes.
Her charge she used.

I know a young lady
Who bought a new belt—
Expensive, she felt,
Still she bought a new belt.
She bought the belt
To dress up the blouse;
She bought the blouse
To accent the skirt;
She bought the skirt
To go with the hose
That prettied and pampered her
Down to her toes.
She bought the hose
To go with the shoes;
To cure her blues,
She bought new shoes.
Her charge she used.

I know a young lady
Who bought a new purse—
You've never seen worse
Than the price of that purse.
She bought the purse
To match the belt;

She bought the belt
To dress up the blouse;
She bought the blouse
To accent the skirt;
She bought the skirt
To go with the hose
That prettied and pampered her
Down to her toes.
She bought the hose
To go with the shoes;
To cure her blues,
She bought new shoes.
Her charge she used.

I know a young lady
Who bought a new hat—
Imagine that,
A pricey new hat.
She bought the hat
To set off the purse;
She bought the purse
To match the belt;
She bought the belt
To dress up the blouse;

She bought the blouse
To accent the skirt;
She bought the skirt
To go with the hose
That prettied and pampered her
Down to her toes.
She bought the hose
To go with the shoes;
To cure her blues,
She bought new shoes.
Her charge she used.

I know a young lady
Who resorted to theft:
She had to—
She had no credit left.

These Grind
Types

These grind types,
These grind types,
They have no fun.
They have no fun.
They're always working till late at night;
They won't even leave work to have a bite;
Somehow their priorities don't seem right;
These grind types.

George E. Porgy

George E. Porgy, corporate spy,
  All the tech he stole was high.
Got stung by the CIA,
  George E. Porgy's in jail today.

The Quarrel

The man I lived with and I fell out.
　　I'll tell you what it 'twas all about.
I had old money and he had none,
　　And that's the way the noise begun.

Bob, Bob, Black Sheep

Bob, Bob, Black Sheep,
   You let the family down,
Burned up your draft card
   And headed out of town.

Fought the establishment,
   Called it all a bore;
Dropped out, loved in,
   Joined the Peace Corps.

Bob, Bob, Black Sheep,
   Where are you today?
You got a job at Merrill Lynch,
   You joined the PTA.

Your hair is trimmed above your ears,
   You bought a spacious house,
Your wardrobe now is from J. Press,
   Instead of Levi Strauss.

You summer at the Vineyard
  In a cottage with your folks.
The wagon that you're driving
  Is a Volvo now—not Volks.

Bob, Bob, Black Sheep,
  Did you just get old?
What could have made a black sheep
  Come back to the fold?

Bob, Bob, Black Sheep,
  To the fold returned.
Did the flame go out?
  Or did you just get burned?

Rub-a-Dub-Dub

Rub-a-dub-dub, let's build a hot tub
   With room for a couple or three,
Using lots of black tile
And bright white cut pile,
   Mirrors heated so they stay fog-free.

It may hurt the fisc,
But we'll add compact disk
   Plus a hookup for wide-screen TV,
And a phone—no, two—one pink, one blue,
   So in contact with brokers we'll be.

Within easy reach
Put a fridge colored peach
   So we'll always have Dom P. on ice
And, yes, my love, add a skylight above
   For in moonlight you always look nice.

Friends will soon beat a path
To try our new bath;
   They'll all know the rules of the tub:
Don't say "Excuse me" when in a Jacuzzi,
   Just rub-a-dub-dub-a-dub-dub.

Now I Buy Me Gold a Heap

Now I buy me gold a heap,
I pray the Lord I bought it cheap.
If it should drop before I wake,
I know my house the bank will take.

Taxes Aren't Simple

Taxes aren't simple,
Taxes aren't quick.
Taxes are so high
It makes me sick.

Mary, Mary, Quite Contrary

Mary, Mary, quite contrary:
  Her corporate cohorts agree—
The word that best describes her
  Has five letters—starts with *b*.

No rings upon her fingers,
  No makeup on her face;
Her suits and hair are all cut square,
  Her favorite perfume? Mace.

She'd never just embarrass you;
  She'd rather bring disgrace.
She'd never stab you in the back;
  She'd do it to your face.

She'd maim to gain more power;
  She'd kill to get more clout.
She has a type of envy
  That Freud once talked about.

And once she gets her claws in
    There's no way to dislodge her.
Mary's style makes Genghis Khan
    Look like Mr. Rogers.

And Mary's male co-workers?
    They more fear than hate her.
Around the cooler Mary's known
    As Ms. Emasculator.

And Ms. she is, not Mrs. —
    She's not one to get mated:
She's lose her power to make men cower
    If her name were hyphenated.

The brass would love to let her go
    But can't risk litigation,
'Cause she'd sue in a heartbeat
    For sex discrimination.

Good Ol' Boy Blue

Good ol' boy Blue, come show your scorn
    For women in business,
    If not those in porn.
Some sexist compulsion
Must drive you to flirt
    With any and everyone
    Dressed in a skirt.

Good ol' boy Blue, pretend you're a god
    Despite cigar ashes
    All over your bod.
Do you think you could manage
To shave once a day?
    Drop a few pounds?
    Trade that mismatched toupee?

Good ol' boy Blue, gone way beyond svelte—
　　Who else wears suspenders
　　To help out his belt?
You sit at your desk
Leaning back in your chair,
　　With massive black wingtips
　　Propped up in the air.

Good ol' boy Blue, you go after results
　　With a mixture of backslap
　　And shouted insults.
And when something really
Just *has* to get done,
　　You call up an ol' boy
　　Who still "owes me one."

Good ol' boy Blue, your main social hub
　　Is an old-fashioned, smoke-filled,
　　All-male eating club.
You go there to drink,
See the guys, and talk sports,
　　But mainly to put down
　　Your female cohorts.

Good ol' boy Blue, your kind's
In retreat:
  Country club connections
  Can't stall your defeat;
Economics demands
We replace aristocracy
  With what you fear most:
  Sex-blind meritocracy.

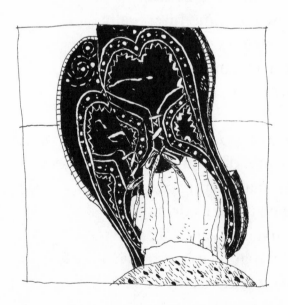

I've Been Working on the Payroll

I've been working on the payroll
    All the livelong day;
I've been working on the payroll
    Just to keep my staff at bay.
Venture capital is tight now
    For a start-up company.
If I want to keep my engineers,
    I'll have to give them equity.

Heigh-ho, Heigh-ho, It's Back to Work I Go

Heigh-ho, heigh-ho,
It's back to work I go.
I had a little baby girl,
So now back to the working world,
Heigh-ho, heigh-ho.

Oh please, oh please,
Don't smear my face with peas.
You little monster, don't you dare!
My God, there's peaches in my hair!
Oh please, oh please.

Oh my, oh my,
Good Lord, that kid can cry.
And teething on my sales reports
Has really got me out of sorts,
Oh my, oh my.

How cute, how cute,
She threw up on my suit.
So now I will be late for work,
I think I'll kill the little jerk,
How cute, how cute.

Five Little Yuppies

This little yuppie played the market;
This little yuppie bought a home;
This little yuppie wined in Paris;
This little yuppie dined in Rome;
This little yuppie cried,
"Please, please, please, give me a loan!"

A Dillar, a Dollar,
a Professional Scholar

A dillar, a dollar,
A professional scholar
With six masters and two Ph.D.'s,
   Plus a quick MBA
   He picked up on the way—
Few thermometers
Have more degrees.

Twelve years and
One hundred grand wasted,
For his learning's
Not yet been applied.
   Though many admire him,
   No one will hire him—
He's overqualified.

Hokey Pokey

You put your
Fat thighs in,
You take your
Fat thighs out,
You put your
Fat thighs in,
And you shake
Them all about.
You do the hokey pokey
Just to try to lose a pound;
That's what
Aerobics is about.

You fill the
Club name in,
You fill the
Club fee out,
You write your
Signature in,
Check by check,
You shell it out.

You do the hokey pokey
Just to try to lose a pound;
That's what
Aerobics is about.

Peter Piper

Peter Piper placed a put
On Phillips Petroleum.
    Projecting picture-perfect profits,
    A put Peter placed.
If Peter Piper placed a put
That promised perfect profits,
    Where are the profits on the put
    That Peter Piper placed?

Three Wise Men of IBM

Three wise men of IBM
   Went out on their own.
If their backing had been stronger,
   My song would be longer.

Wee Willie Winkie

Wee Willie Winkie
Runs through the town
Uphill and downhill,
Always poundin' ground.
A Walkman on his head
Puts rhythm in his feet;
He turns on Tina Turner
And he's fleet to the beat.
Willie is pure muscle—
He has no body fat;
Anytime he gains a pound
He runs it off like that.
And Willie is so straight,
It makes you want to cry;
His sole turn-on is suiting up
And catching runner's high.
He's even sworn off sex—
His mistress is the road.
He only stops to sleep
(And, of course, to carbo-load).

Wee Willie Winkie's in
A marathon a week;
He ran his last in 2:09
And hasn't reached his peak.
Willie claims he runs because
It's crucial to his psyche
But it's really 'cause he wants to get
Endorsement bucks from Nike.

Birds of a Feather

Birds of a feather flock together,
To the Hamptons and Newport they fly,
    Where the crowd is superb
    And summer's a verb
And you'd no sooner be poor than die.

Birds of a feather fret over whether
They're wearing the proper Vuarnets.
    They dress like peacocks,
    Walk around with no socks
In a Tanqueray G&T haze.

Birds of a feather worry 'bout weather
For golfing and tennis and sailing.
    But when it snows,
    They just use their nose
And practice the sport of inhaling.

Birds of a feather flock together
And the old pecking orders run deep.
   You must fit in by birth
   Or total net worth—
Social status does not come cheap, cheap.

Two Firms in Kilkenny

There once were two firms in Kilkenny;
Each thought there was one firm too many.
So they fought and they fit
And slashed prices a bit
Till, excepting their names
And their officers' shames,
Instead of two firms there weren't any.

Little Miss Muffles

Little Miss Muffles
   Sat eating truffles,
Pâté de foie gras and Brie.
   Along came a writer
   Who tried to invite her
To his co-op, his etchings to see.

This caused poor Miss Muffles
   To choke on her truffles;
Then sweetly she said to the chap,
   "Pardon me if this will
   On your plans put a chill,"
As she poured her Chablis in his lap.

Lean Cuisine

Lean Cuisine hot,
Lean Cuisine cold,
Lean Cuisine nine days straight
Gets a little old.
Some eat it hot,
Some eat it cold,
Some eat it left over—
That's a little bold.

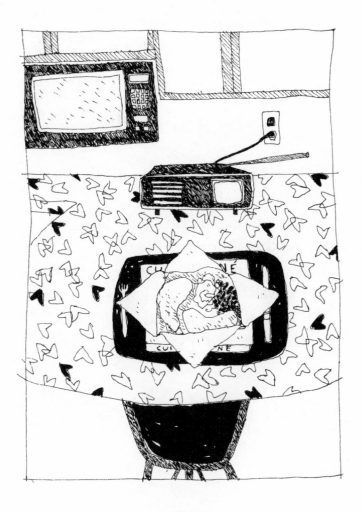

Jack and Jill

Jack and Jill went up the hill
    To ski another run.
Jack hit a tree and broke his knee
    But that didn't end the fun.
Jack didn't hate his lodge-bound state;
    He was happy as could be—
For all that week he and Jill did seek
    The joys of *après ski*.

So You Own a Boat

(Why row, row, row when you can sail?)

So you own a boat
Sixty feet abeam,
Marry me, marry me,
Marry me, marry me!
Life will be a dream.

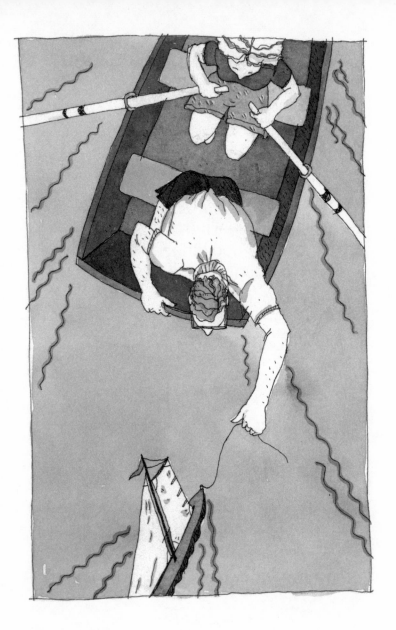

For Want of Fresh Basil

For want of fresh basil,
My sauce is a loss;
For want of good sauce,
My pasta's disasta';
For want of good pasta,
My dinner's no winner;
For want of good dinner,
Romance has no chance;
For want of romance,
This old maid won't get laid—
And all for the want of fresh basil.

Itsy-Bitsy Diaper

The itsy-bitsy diaper
Soaked up the baby's spout.
Down came her mom,
Who threw the diaper out.
If she changed another,
She swore she'd go insane;
Then the itsy-bitsy diaper
Soaked up the spout again…

Humpty-Dumpty

Humpty-Dumpty, seven feet tall,
Humpty-Dumpty sure can play ball.
All the cum laudes in college today
Never will match Humpty's after-tax pay.

Tweedledum and Tweedledee

Tweedledum and Tweedledee
   Resolved to have a baby,
For Tweedledum said Tweedledee
   Would soon be too old, maybe.

So Tweedledee went off the pill
   And for three months they waited.
Their anxious palms were sweaty,
   Their eager breaths were bated.

The big night came, they drank champagne,
    And then to make their blood boil
They watched a rented porn flick
    And microwaved the Love Oil.

Day after day, way after way,
    It really was unbelievable
The crazy things the Tweedles tried
    To make Tweedledee conceivable.

But this was no mere casual sex,
    For they'd read studies relating
The selection of baby's gender
    To timely copulating.

For girls, you make love early;
    For boys, you do it late.
This assumes you can predict
    The ovulation date.

And *that* you do through little bits
    Of voodoo, science, and art,
Plus checking daily secretions
    And the Basal Temperature Chart.

To birth a bouncing baby boy
    All known techniques they tried,
With thermometer, pH test kit,
    And computer by their side.

They input all the data
    (Cross-checked beyond a doubt),
And when they got the output,
    They knew when to put out.

And now they have a baby boy—
    Live proof that pregnancies
Can be controlled by learning
    About the birds and the PC's.

Cabbage Patch, Cabbage Patch

Cabbage Patch, Cabbage Patch,
   Get 'em while you can.
Every child wants one
   All across the land.
Yes, they are expensive,
   But yes, of course you'll pay,
For until your child gets one
   You'll feel guilt each day.

Sing a Song of Past Tense

Sing a song of past tense
   About a former I,
Before aplenty fatfoods
   Shot my weight sky-high.

When my weight was lower,
   I'd eat most anything.
I'd start each day by scarfing down
   A nut-filled Danish ring.

But I soon was nearly fainting
   For bagels and cream cheese.
The thought of David's Cookies
   Would bring me to my knees.

Something light for lunch, you say?
   I knew just the thing!
Why not have a dainty dish
   Down at Burger King?

On the way back to the job
　　I would without fail pause
For hot fudge over chocolate chip
　　Down at Häagen Dazs.

Afternoons were tougher;
　　By the snack machine I'd stay.
Somehow I always made it through
　　On Cokes and Milky Way.

At dinnertime I'd place a call:
　　"Your largest pizza, please,
Smother it with everything—
　　Except for anchovies."

Alas, all that's behind me now
　　And I'm no longer trim.
Today my daily intake
　　Is one glass of Nutra-Slim.

My First Kid

My first kid, when he's one,
Will know the works of Mendelssohn,
With a nick-nack paddy-wack,
Oh, how he has grown!
My first kid is not a drone.

My first kid, when he's two,
Will write in Latin and Greek, too.
With a nick-nack paddy-wack,
Oh, how he has grown!
My first kid is not a drone.

My first kid, when he's three,
Will finish his first Ph.D.
With a nick-nack paddy-wack,
Oh, how he has grown!
My first kid is not a drone.

My first kid, when he's four,
Will map uncharted ocean floor.
With a nick-nack paddy-wack,
Oh, how he has grown!
My first kid is not a drone.

My first kid, when he's five,
Will patent a new hard disk drive.
With a nick-nack paddy-wack,
Oh, how he has grown!
My first kid is not a drone.

My first kid, when he's six,
Will start at center for the Knicks.
With a nick-nack paddy-wack,
Oh, how he has grown!
My first kid is not a drone.

My first kid, when he's seven,
Will own a summer place in Devon.
With a nick-nack paddy-wack,
Oh, how he has grown!
My first kid is not a drone.

My first kid, when he's eight,
Will counsel several heads of state.
With a nick-nack paddy-wack,
Oh, how he has grown!
My first kid is not a drone.

My first kid, when he's nine,
Will be a connoisseur of wine.
With a nick-nack paddy-wack,
Oh, how he has grown!
My first kid is not a drone.

My first kid, when he's ten,
The novel of the age will pen.
With a nick-nack paddy-wack,
Oh, how he has grown!
My first kid is not a drone.

Young Mother Goose

Young Mother Goose,
When she wants to fly,
    Drives a new BMW 535i.
And when Simple Simon
Comes home from his job,
    He hits the highway
    In his new Turbo Saab.
While little Ms Muffet sits
With someone beside her
    In her Alfa Romeo
    Convertible Spyder.
And when Tweedledum drives
To get Tweedledee
    He jumps in their brand-new
    Jaguar XKE.
Jack Sprat goes from work
Back to his home address
    In his shiny new red Peugeot 505 S.

Bo-Peep makes her homeward-bound
Day-end farewell,
  Then drives her
  Mercedes 380 SL.
They hop in machines
That go speeds most unlawful,
  Then sit still for hours
  'Cause traffic is awful.

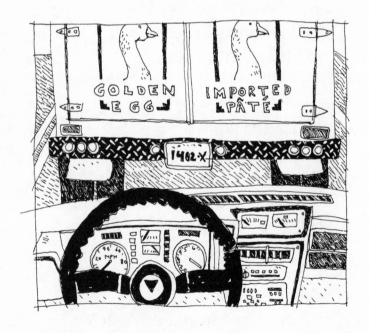